Yes

the Holy Spirit

Spoke to Me, Too

My Book of Poems, Songs, Sermons

and Short Story

glory j mitz

Yes the Holy Spirit Spoke to Me, Too

glory j mitz

Quotations marked KJV are from the King James Version of the Bible.

ISBN -13-978-0578-40749-4

DEDICATION

To William, who did not understand the change in his mom, but who still believed as best as he could, that she was called into GOD's ministry, even when he saw her, go through some very hard times.

To Yabette, who is steadfast and always there.

To all my sisters in Christ, who are so faithful to the call, even when they are not sure of what their very own calling is. They still press in.

To all the Teachers at SEBTS, who taught and teach in the Women's Ministry program. Thank you for your dedication to the Word of GOD and for being a wonderful example to all, who attend the classes at SEBTS.

To Belinda, who listen to me faithfully, talk about the Word Of GOD, every day at lunch for over 2 years.

Finally, to Pastor L. I miss those trips across our jobs campus to get to your office. I have tears over the opportunity I did not see.

ACKNOWLEGMENT

William Donnell, thank you for your kindness and all the support you have given me over these last 12 years.

Thank You Jennifer, for those words of encouragement on reading my very first manuscript.

Thanks Vicky. Loved your card and comments.

PREFACE

Some may say this is a very simple book. It is a collection of the words given to me by The Holy Spirit. I didn't understand that initially. All I knew, was suddenly, I would have all these words in my mind and my thoughts. I am so thankful to the Teachers at SEBTS, in Wake Forest, NC. They taught me about The Holy Spirit and how he speaks to us. They also taught on how important it is to write down what is given to us, by The Holy Spirit. They call it journaling.

I now understand that He (The Holy Spirit) is the one who gives all of us our gifts, skills and talents. Some use theirs for the World, while we as Christians are to use ours to glorify GOD and His Kingdom.

I didn't know, as I was journaling, that I would one day want to compile all those sermons, notes and words together in a book!

Yes, to some, this may seem to be a simple little book, not much excitement, but even still, it is powerful, to GOD BE THE GLORY!

INTRODUCTION

We usher, we sing in choirs, we do missionary work, hospitality, and so much more in church, but still there is this longing to know, "what am 'I ' called to do?"

May you find the answer to that question. There in, is your ministry (at least one of them), that GOD has so graciously given to you to do. It is not for you to leave your church, but it is to help you, encourage others in the Faith. Those in your church and most importantly, it is for us to help those who are outside the Kingdom of GOD.

Some of you are Prophetess, Evangelist, Preachers, Teachers, Christian Book Writers, Christian Song Writers, Christian Actors, Christian Activist, Christian Beauticians, Christian Doctors, Christian Nurses, Chaplains, Christian Poets, etc. The list just goes on and on. Please remember The Holy Spirit gives us our gifts, skills and talents and he give them to us, severally, to be used for the Kingdom of GOD.

The reason for this book is to show how The Holy Spirit worked on me. He has given me so much, I have written it down, as best as I could right now. Praise GOD!

It seems to me that The Holy Spirit is often forgotten about. He is there for us, to guide us, lead us in the right direction, to always bring us to the Truth, which is Jesus Christ. Everything he does is to lead us to Jesus Christ. We are to invoke the power of the Holy Spirit by calling on him. I call on him a lot. I ask that he dwell in me richly, and that I have a double portion of his power. I thank GOD for sending us The Holy Spirit. He (The Holy Spirit) is awesome, as is our Lord and Savior Jesus Christ!

We have been called, to be a light to others (wherever the Lord needs us to go, may we go by the power of The Holy Spirit). It is called: The Great Commission (Matthew 28: 18-20) (KJV).

My poems are very easy to read. A few are extremely interesting, like “We Walk Among Them”.

I love the song: Jesus, He is Lord of Everything.

All things in this book are for encouragement. The entire book is to encourage you in the things of our LORD Jesus Christ.

In my short story you will find that Courtney was called by GOD to be in the Fivefold Ministry. It talks briefly about her struggles to do what GOD had ordained her to do.

She laid everything on the altar, despite her feelings of loneliness or of being unaccepted. No one understood where she was going or what she was about, but she held on to this thought: The world looks at the outer appearance, but GOD looks at the heart. 1Sam 16:7 (KJV)

The sermons are very insightful. I am so amazed at what the Lord GOD has given me. I wanted to write everything just the way it was given to me. That way no one can say oh, she is trying to be so intellectual. This is about The Holy Spirit and our Lord Jesus Christ. It is not about me. Please read the book slowly, take it all in, enjoy it, then share.

My Testimony is non-Fiction. It truly happened to me and here is the dichotomy for me. It was one of the most wonderful experiences I have had. I didn't remember anything about this side while I was there in heaven. Seems I had peace. Most importantly, I did not look the same, my body had changed.

It also, became one of the most frightening experiences I have had, once I woke up or to put it another way, was sent back. It frightened me so bad, I could not sleep in my bed for two weeks, because I knew I had died, and I didn't fully understand just what had happened to me.

This book is my witnessing tool, for the LORD Jesus Christ and the Kingdom of GOD. My prayer is that many will read it and their hearts be touched and or their eyes opened. In Jesus Precious and Holy Name. Amen!

Yes the Holy Spirit Spoke to Me, Too

Table of Contents

CHAPTER 1: POEMS

TO GOD, MY FATHER

HOME SWEET HOME HOME SWEET HOME!

Sweet home, my quiet place
I want to thank you LORD.
My tears are turning to joy for your Love and Grace.

I thank you.
My heart is full of happiness!
My heart no longer aches - Thank You God
Thank You all my days.

HOME SWEET HOME HOME SWEET HOME!

Sweet Home, my quiet place
Thank GOD, all my days
glory j mitz / 07- 31 – 03

THE LORD SAYS...

WALK WITH ME, TALK WITH ME. LET ME SEE HOW YOU ARE

STAY WITH ME, PRAY WITH ME. LET ME SEE YOUR HOLY PLAN

STAY WITH ME, THEN YOU WILL SEE HOW WONDERFUL THIS LIFE CAN BE

WALK WITH ME, TALK WITH ME. LOVE ME, STAY WITH ME

AND YOU WILL SEE HOW WONDERFUL LIFE CAN BE

glory j mitz / 01-25-06

FROM THE BACK OF THE BUS

Came the Freedom of today
GOD was able to see separation, oppression
dislike and high mindedness

Came the desire to have more, to be more
to no longer be hungry, poor, humiliated,
hated and disliked

Came strength, humbleness, love of GOD
and the fellowman
Came the willingness to die, to be beat,
even thrown in jail (or talked about)
if it meant Freedom from bondage

Came an understanding of those who
sit at the front, for they only have a
view of themselves
Came the ability to see the whole
world for what it is

From the back of the bus
Came those in rags, wanting a better life
Came those looking for GOD. From the
Back of The Bus, GOD delivered us.   Amen!

glory jean mitz / 04-14-08

WITH LOVE

With love all Things Grow
With love all Things Flourish
With love no Things Perish
I showed you great and wonderful things, with
Love
I bring you home to me, with Love
I would set all things as they should be, because I
am Love!
A house on a hill, a new place
Red Bricks, Circle Drive this is your home.
Brand new from me to you. A house on a hill
with Love

glory j mitz / 12-10-11

WEEP NOT FOR THE THINGS OF OLD

Weep not for the things of Old, but

Weep deeply for the Blessing therein.

The dawning of a new Day, the moment, that moment!

WHEN LIGHT FIRST CAME IN....

The moment, that moment, when you first saw the SAVIOR'S face:

The moment, that moment, when you beheld The Savior's Loving Grace.

glory j mitz / 08-2011

HE'S BEEN WITH ME

He's been with me
He'll be with you
There's nothing he can't do
There's nothing my GOD can't do

He's been with me all my days
He's been with me in times of misery
He's been with me in all ways
HE'S BEEN WITH ME
He's perfect in every way
He just wants your Love and Praise

He's been with me, through the years
In my joy and my fears

glory j mitz / 01-14-2012

You're So Good, Your Wonderful

You're So Good, Your Wonderful
There's no place I would rather be, then in your company
My eyes are on you only!
My heart beats for you
You are precious in my sight
I am so glad you gave me Life.
There's nothing I wouldn't do for you

glory j mitz / 03-03-2012 at 4:02amE

SOMEONE WAS CALLING ME!

Someone was Calling me!
I didn't know from which direction it came.

Someone was Calling me!
I could not see it, but like a mighty wind, it
began to move me along

Someone was Calling me!
It was like a song, I heard in the early morn, then
stayed on my mind, all day long
Someone was Calling me!
So, Finally I said - here I am!!
What do you want?
What do you need me to do?
Someone was Calling me!
My Father, My GOD, My Lord and Savior, Jesus
Christ. I'm so glad it was you!

glory j mitz / 02-11-2012

WE WALK AMONG THEM

We walk among them!

We are Robed in Red

Our outer garment is a Robe of Red

There is a cross, white, placed over the Heart area

We wear head bands that read: Logos, The Word, Rhema

Underneath the Red Robes, that are Brilliant in color, are garments of white, that illuminate great brightness, whenever the Robe is open.

We walk among them!

In our right hand is a Lantern, with an exceeding Bright Light

It illuminates anything that stands near it.

It is and we are, a Reflection of the ONE who sent us.

Its brilliance can be seen from afar off, so all who see it is drawn near

All who step into the light are changed from darkness to look or resemble the Light.

We walk among them!

Waving our Lanterns to and fro, calling out to those hidden, entrapped by the darkness.

In our left hand is the Book of Wisdom, explanation, our compass

It explains the Light, the direction to use, to lead those in darkness to the Light.

Our paths are set. We hear them calling to us, to help them.

They didn't know that their cries of mourning, whaling, uncertainty, loneliness, of being lost, are calls to us. We are driven, we must follow the call, set before us.

Our feet are covered with shoes that look more like socks, but with extremely strong, flexible bottom soles. The shoes are cotton that stretches. We walk softly, but confident in any type of terrain, for the soles are strong and flexible.

We call out: He is calling you. Step into the glorious Light. Feel the warmth of the Light!

We call out: He is calling you. Follow us!

We walk among them!

They are afraid, they do not recognize us. We are foreign to them. They have never really had their mind's eye open before, just lived in the darkness of their minds. They see us and are afraid, but the warmth of The Light draws them close, then closer.

They see themselves for the first time, their eyes have been closed. They have on **Robes of Chains**.

On the Chains, which cover their bodies all over, are words that say: Sin Rules here: Hunger, hate, poverty, jealousy, loneliness, alienation, despair, no freedom, death and on the lock that holds the Chain, are subscribed these Words: **OWNED BY SATAN**.

We walk among them!

Waving our Lanterns, carrying our Book of Wisdom, calling out to them. He, the Light is calling you!

The Holy Spirit

Step into The Glorious Light. Be Not Afraid....

They step into The Glorious Light. The Chain starts to crack and break down one link, then another.

Their mind's eye opens fully, their hands become free. They walk closer and closer to the Light, until the chain is gone, the lock has fallen off.

Their Robe is Changed into a Bright Brilliant Red!

We walk among them!

glory j mitz / 10-17-2014 at 1pmEastern

Will We Dance, This Dance for All Eternity?

Will We Dance, This Dance, For All Eternity?

Is it you and me? Am I the one?

Am I the one you think I am?

The one you love.

We won't pass this way again

We won't dance the path again

You must be sure, Is it you and me?

Love is so wonderful, it never ceases

Even so, people end and stop

Love never really cease.

glory j mitz / 2013 or 2014

Every Where I go

Everywhere I go, it shall be yours

Every place my feet touch, shall be mine and I am yours.

So everywhere I go, shall belong to you - Father.

Everywhere my feet touch, I shall proclaim your Holy name

Everywhere I go, shall belong to you, for I am yours, and you said everywhere my feet touch, will be mine. Amen!

glory j mitz / 06-17-2015

CHAPTER 2: MY SONGS

TODAY

OH, THERE IS A WAY A WAY
OH, THERE IS A WAY A WAY

OH, THERE IS A WAY A WAY, TODAY.

THERE IS A LOVE. THERE IS A LOVE
OH, THERE IS A LOVE, A LOVE TODAY!

OH, MY LORD! OH YES, MY LORD!
OH, THERE IS A WAY TO THE LORD TO
DAY.

glory j mitz / 10-15-06

HE

He Lives deep down in my heart
He Gives me peace and joy
He Rules all of me
He Loves everyone
He Lives day to day

GOD Reigns in every way
GOD Loves everyone
GOD Gave his only son
He Loves all of me
He Reigns in my heart

glory j mitz / 2009

There's Only One Way to Heaven

There's only one Road you can take

1) There's one way
There's one way
There's one way

2) You can go
You can go
You can go

and the Road is Jesus Christ

There is only one way to Heaven and the Road is Jesus Christ!

glory j mitz / 01/24/2010

My Christmas Song to C'Niiya

If I could give you anything, a part of me. It
would be for you to love Jesus whole heartedly
For he will give you all you ever need.

If I could show you what I would like for you to
see.

It would be me on my knees, praying for you,
your Dad and me
For prayer is all you will ever need.

If I could touch your mind. It would be for you
to study GOD, for he is most kind.

For he loved us so much. He gave us all we
need. His Son and Heir of Thee.
glory j mitz / 12/22/ year not known

JESUS, HE IS LORD OF EVERYTHING

Jesus, Jesus

Adonai, Messiah, Emmanuel, Elohim.

He is Lord of Everything!

Jesus, Jesus

Rose of Sharon, Balm of Gilead, King of Kings,

Lord of Lords, Ruler of Rulers.

He is Lord of All things!

Jesus, Jesus

Ancient of Days, Alpha and Omega, The Beginning and The End.

He is LORD of All Men!

He is LORD

He is LORD

He is LORD

HE IS LORD OF EVERYTHING!

HE IS LORD

HE IS LORD

HE IS LORD

HE IS LORD OF EVERYTHING!

Amein

Amen!

glory j mitz / 12/19/2010

You will be my Loving Little Girl!

I love you; I need you, Forever

I want to share your Love with the World

I want to be your Loving little girl!

I love you Father, how tender you are

I need to go into the World.

You will! Be My Loving Little Girl

glory j mitz / 03/19/2012 at 8:07pmE

glory mitz

You are the great I Am

You are Almighty GOD

You are all I ever need

The greatest, the best, the one I love the most

The Everlasting Rock

Forever More (high) Forever More (low) Forever More

glory j mitz / 7/30/2012 at 9:53pmE

CHAPTER 3: SERMONS

What A Mighty Adversary Death Was

I began to understand what a mighty adversary Death was, as I thought on the word: "impossible".

When reading in the Bible about the Resurrection of Jesus Christ and how we will rise with him on his second coming (1 THESS 4: 11-18). It reminded me of what we have hoped for. To overcome the "impossible". Death. When we see our love ones lying in their coffins, we are brought face to face with that opponent (Death) and His cruelty is made evident.

We see the body, cold and hard as a rock. How appalling for us, to come to the realization that this is our fate as well. No breath of life. A body, hard as rock. A sepulcher with no escape.

It's finality. We mourn for our love ones, but the other side is, we understand that this too is our fate. We know that we cannot beat Death.

Oh, but we do try, in a vain attempt: I will eat better, I will alleviate stress from my life.

I will be kind or as the ones, that are truly lost say; I will live life to its fullest, as if this will defeat him.

But Jesus Christ Came!

Jesus Christ, our LORD and SAVIOR, gave Death a mighty, mighty blow. He brought Death to its own death and He (Jesus Christ) only, rose to tell us about it. (1 Cor 15: 53-58) What a mighty GOD we serve.

Death being death requires it all. Like the Flesh, it wants what it wants and who can stop him?

For we in and of ourselves have not the power to stop or change any order that GOD has established.

The Death card was not intended for us and so it became a mighty weapon against us. Death requires SIN. WE were not created sinful, initially, but all are now born into a (sinful) fallen world. Death a spiritual verdict for the fallen Angels, had a massive impact upon us, the Sons of GOD.

Originally, we were created to be like GOD our Father. The Bible tells us, we were created in his image. (Genesis 1: 27 & 28) (KJV).

Death meant separation from GOD, eternally. It was meant for the Angels who rebelled, not us. For us it meant our Spirits being eternally separated from GOD, and eventually the death of the bodies we inhabit, as well. A double (whammy) blow for us, and since it was not meant for us initially, there is no way for us alone to conquer over death. Death's grip, his hold, is too strong for us.

The reality of all this, is when we stand facing the shell of our loved ones, as the body lies helpless in the casket. Our mourning is a cry for help, a terrible wrong has been done. We know this but cannot stop or change it. So, on two fronts we needed deliverance from Death.

Thank GOD for his SON, JESUS CHRIST!

Jesus has come as deliverer of our Souls and the Redeemer of our bodies. It is through him, that a great wrong is made right. Our Father is a GOD of Order. He had set death over rebellious Spiritual Beings, first.

It was for Satan and his followers. Those that rebelled against GOD, initially. So, Satan had to "by order" cause us "first" to become separated spiritually from GOD (The Fall of Adam and Eve) (Genesis 3: 1-24) (KJV). Only then could Satan have power over us and be able to destroy us physically (bodily).

What a Mighty GOD we serve. Thank you, LORD JESUS, for saving us!

Our God knew he had to "by order" the same way we fell, we had to be restored. First Spiritually back to GOD, then we could live on forever as intended, by GOD and with GOD.

Reason alone for The CROSS and the RESURRECTION.

The Blood of Jesus removes our sin, because he was Sinless. He Rose, so we can rise in him and through his power, we will have new bodies. We will live forever in Christ Jesus.

He is the Power, because he knew no Sin. He died sinless. Death was not established for the SINLESS, and therefore, it had no sting on Jesus Christ, no power. Death becomes not, through our LORD and SAVIOR JESUS CHRIST.

Death could not hold him. He became Ruler over Death. He alone has the Keys to Hades and Death. (Revelation 1: 18) (KJV)

He is Ruler of Rulers, Lord of Lords, King of Kings, Life Everlasting. Amen

glory j mitz / 09-01-10 at 4:53amE

CHURCH HISTORY

Question: Why Study the History of The Church?

I believe it is man's attempt (by God's power) to summarize God's mighty work. From the giving of a rainbow in the sky (Genesis 9:11-17, a token) (KJV) to the foundations of the earth, being torn apart, the sun turning dark, and the stars falling from the sky (Revelation 6: 12-17).

We understand, we are created, not knowing the past. Each new generation is created looking ahead to their own future. Therein, not knowing GOD or who he is and his glorious works.

We must know the History of our church to solidify who our GOD is. He, himself set the foundation for his Church and its history, by giving us The Holy Bible.

With his mighty hand, he continues to write the story down as it progresses by having man, write down those marvelous events, of Church happenings in each generation. I believe right up until the very last moment, here on earth, GOD will still inspire someone to write the story down.

From symbols on clay jars, to papaya, to wood paper, to radio, to TV, and for my generation the Internet. The history of his Church is really written in every man's heart, for it is the Love of Christ, which we know cannot be contained within, but must be given out.

An expression of GOD, for the next generation.

The History of his Church is his story. (1 John 4:7-8) (KJV)

It is His testimony of who he is, to each new generation!

glory j mitz / 09-02-10 at 2:09pmE

LORD JESUS, HELP ME TO REMEMBER

We as Godly Women, cannot just do church or church culture, (a term I am setting aside for this message). What I mean is, doing only that which is specific to our own churches, never stepping outside of the Church doors.

We are very cultural, that is, we identify ourselves by people groups. Some groups may like potato salad, with collard greens or another will do just salads. Still others, meat and pastas, like lasagna, stuffed ricotta, etc. We identify our people groups by the way we live, and it is wonderful, and yes, other people groups may like some of the things specific to yours or another people group.

We are the same in our churches too. I have visited different denominational groups in Raleigh, Durham, Wilson. Each church has its own culture (things that are specific to that Church group).

My examples are these: I went to a Pentecostal (Holiness) church (a couple to be exact). They would sing for a couple of hours, then preach for another hour. For the 1st hour I was hanging in there with them, singing, then I got tired, but they were still going strong. It was all good, I enjoyed it, but I just could not sing and shout that long. So, I began to understand that is specific to Pentecostal (Holiness) Churches.

I also, went to a Methodist Church and they were lighting the candles, kneeling for prayer and I loved that too, but it wasn't who I was completely. I needed something more.

Finally, I was at the Baptist Churches and they prayed a lot, with some singing, some shouting. I heard long sermons and loved it. I knew in my heart I wanted to be at the Baptist church.

I want to say that I love all the above. I believe GOD gave all the above to us to use, so he would be edified in all ways: prayer, praise and symbols. That way we could not idolized one way of worship over another.

Everything is to be all about him, nothing lost. Now to get to the specific of all Churches. We all have the praise team, the usher board, the first aid ministry, the music ministry and the missionary ministry. You get the point, and as good as Sunday morning is. It is not enough.

I love Sunday mornings; I live for Sundays. I love my church and church family. I am blessed to have been called out of the World, to serve GOD and so are you blessed, also. You have been called out of the World to serve GOD and him only, as he has directed us.

So even though we serve in Church (which is a joy for us), we are to remember to serve in the communities wherever there is a need. God reminded me of this. He let me see the needs of others. That is, what Christianity is really all about.

As we do Church and Church Culture, let us remember to do the same thing in the communities. Luke 10 - Good Samaritan / Jesus washing the disciple's feet (John 13: 14-15) (KJV).

Finally, LOVE. Everything is done in Love for the Father; As GOD is Love (1 John 3: 9-10) (KJV)

We all need to be like Peter, who stepped out of the boat. Yes, he started to sink but at least he believed in the Lord enough to try to walk on the water. The others just sat in the boat. Amen

glory j mitz / 01/29/11 at 8:41amE

CHAPTER 4: MY SHORT STORY

GOD's LITTLE CHAPEL ON THE HILL

BY

glory j mitz

Romans 5: 1-5 (KJV)

THEREFORE, BEING JUSTIFIED BY FAITH WE HAVE PEACE WITH GOD, THROUGH OUR LORD JESUS CHRIST:

BY WHOM ALSO WE HAVE ACCESS BY FAITH INTO THIS GRACE WHERE WE STAND AND REJOICE IN HOPE OF THE GLORY OF GOD.

AND NOT ONLY SO, BUT WE GLORY IN TRIBULATIONS ALSO: KNOWING THAT TRIBULATION WORKETH PATIENCE;

AND PATIENCE, EXPERIENCE; AND EXPERIENCE, HOPE:

AND HOPE MAKETH NOT ASHAMED; BECAUSE THE LOVE OF GOD IS SHED ABROAD IN OUR HEARTS BY THE HOLY GHOST WHICH IS GIVEN UNTO US.

AMEN!

Let no man or situation cause you to Stumble.
Keep your eyes Forever Fixed on the Cross.
There in is your Salvation!

TRUST IN THE LORD!

THIS LIFE: IS NOT MY OWN

Courtney Louise was dressed in an all-white, linen outfit. A long white linen skirt, with a white linen top. Her earrings and necklace were blue like the heavens above. On her left hand where 3 rings: one was a seminary ring, another: the sovereignty ring, that spoke of God's sovereignty in her life. The 3rd ring was a wedding ring, that had been given to her years ago and never used. The blue high heels she wore, they were mostly strapping that crisscrossed across the front of the foot. The shoes added eloquence to her outfit.

Her hair, all gray now, with only one or two black streaks along the front. She wore it kind of wild, almost like a large afro from the sixty's but it is curly and long. Her skin is of a fine texture, as she had aged it had gotten thinner, but her face was still young and youthful looking. Her brown eyes still big and bright as when she was fourteen. Her skin color was a smooth, satiny brown like the Indians of India.

She was told (because she was taken in as a foster child at age one and didn't know her family) that her grandmother on her father's side was a Ma lotto. Her grandmother on her mother's side was ½ Cherokee and had come from the Indian's that lived near Pineville, South Carolina. It was reported that her grandmother on her father's side had been one of the prettiest women in Enfield, NC.

Courtney was elegant, a woman of grace, a Women of GOD! Quiet and reserved, except when it came to the word of GOD. She could never get enough of talking about the Lord or his Kingdom. This day was special, as she, was being recognized as the Interim Pastor of the church. This time with the grace of GOD, she was the one being recognized. Usually it was someone else being recognized, but not today.

This had not been her vision, but seem to have been placed upon her, given the times and financials of the Church.

Yes, it was a small to mid-size church. To some, this was not so much of a big deal, but to her, her very life was brought into existence for this one purpose. To honor God, to exalt God, to proclaim him as King, Lord and Savior. This had started as a ministry to women; those who had been abused, abandon, or were just hurting. It had evolved into her being one of the associate pastors and now Interim Pastor.

She sat in Church in her usual spot, waiting, but today she was waiting with anticipation. She had cried a lot leading up to today, some of the tears were of joy and some of sadness.

Other people could not understand the intensity that she felt for GOD's word or wanting to live a life as faithful as she could to the call that she had been called to. For she knew it was God's love, and his love only, that had protected her and brought her this far.

It had not been an easy journey. She had not fully understood it herself, until about 5 years into it. Then she began to understand that something more had happened. She was driven by what she wasn't sure of, at first. Only time, revealed it was God's Plan for her life.

It wasn't that she had chosen this for herself, she thought she would be a beauty salon owner. Having people come into her salon, where she would share the Word of God with them, while she was working on their hair. She had heard it said, "If you don't think God has a sense of humor, tell GOD your plans for your life".

God had made it very clear, through a series of test and dreams that this was what he wanted for her. A life devoted to him and service to his Kingdom.

THE MOMENT! THAT MOMENT

The life she lived now was totally different then it was before That Moment! The life she lived before had no substance, no real meaning. No one cared for her, not really. She understood that now. She was an "it" person, not really belonging to anyone. If something needed to be done for her foster parents, she was it.

If her husband needed money, she was it. If he needed his clothes washed or a meal fixed, she was it. She washed dishes for her foster parents, scrub floors, went to the supermarket for them, and sadly her marriage had the same dynamics.

It was just yesterday, she sat in her study room at home, alone, wishing there was one, just one, who loved her enough to attend this special event with her.

Oh, she knew Elder Hightown and his wife, Mary, would be there.

They were her family now, but she was thinking of having someone there, who was special to her and her to him, but there wasn't anyone. There hadn't been anyone else in a long time.

She often thought about that life. That life, she had lived, before That Special Moment, had no real love. It was about the natural, the world's way of thinking. People using others for money or seeing them as a commodity to their problems. The life she lived after That Special Moment, with God's grace was spiritual, not perfect, but Spiritual. Her looking for and desiring in her heart the things of GOD.

That great Hope of things to come. (Genesis 3:15) She thought of that poem that God gave to her early one morning, years ago. It spoke of that Special Moment. It was just one of many poems, songs and sermons that God had given to her over the years, by the power of the Holy Spirit.

He would wake her up early in the morning hours. She would be given words (poems, songs and sermons). She didn't understand the power of what was happening to her at first, then she was taught (at the seminary she had attended) that it was GOD speaking to her.

She was taught that she must write it down right then or later the words would be totally gone from her memory, just like a dream that was so vivid while dreaming it, but upon awakening, not able to remember any of it.

This one she wrote down, as with many others after that, but this one explained That Moment:

Weep not for the things of Old but weep deeply for the Blessing therein.

The dawning of a new day, The Moment, That Moment! When Light first came in! The Moment, That Moment, when you first saw the Savior's face;

The Moment, That Moment, when you beheld The Saviors Loving Grace.

This poem happened after reading about our Lord Jesus Christ going before Pilate. Peter being in the courtyard and upon hearing the Rooster crow, Jesus looked at Peter (as described in the book of LUKE). It says Peter wept bitterly, because he remembered what Jesus had told him. That he would deny him 3 times before the rooster crowed. (Luke 22: 54-62) (KJV)

Those words "wept bitterly" had stayed with her. She remembered how after giving her life to Christ, she found herself weeping bitterly. For she realized that she too was a sinner (wanting revenge on her ex-husband, for all he had done to her). Her not wanting to forgive her parents, but GOD showed her, his love, mercy and his saving grace. She wept bitterly, understanding how much grace GOD had showed her, by saving her.

AARON FLOWERS

As she had sat in her office, yesterday, Saturday morning, her mind had raced back over time. She must have been there for hours, but it seemed like it was just minutes.

She remembered Aaron Flowers. A good man, a Godly man. He was one of the Reverends at the church when she first joined, years ago. She had fallen in love with him and it seemed at one time that he too loved her. She really believed he did at first. The age difference of 6 years didn't appear to matter. She knows now, that time, the issues of life and their ministries were hard on him and their relationship.

He was a newly appointed Reverend back then, full of energy, into everything (outreach, young men's ministry, helping greet the new people who came in). He was on fire for the Lord. While, her ministry to the women was just getting started.

She even remembered the moment she fell in love with him. He walked past her one Sunday, after church to fellowship with a couple of the people in the congregation. She noticed those deep-set dimples, skin smooth and blemish free. A beautiful brown bronze complexion. Eyes wide and bright, even his pearly white teeth, were beautiful to her behind that smile. Yes, he was a gorgeous man. Shoulders broad, he had a slow confident walk about him, as if he was analyzing every person and letting every person analyze him. She always knew she was on his radar, even if he never really talked to her personally.

It took about 6 months before he would talk to her directly. He would at first, just give her the eye and look at her intensely. So much so that all she could do eventually was smile. One day he smiled back at her, too. After that, they became good friends. He loved cars, kids and GOD more than anything. In time, as she got to know him better, she fell even more in love with Aaron Flowers.

THE CHURCH ON THE OTHER SIDE

Over time, she realized she had hurt him, not fully understanding him, nor his needs. It wasn't intentional. She had to do what GOD had called her to do, but she had made everything about her. He really needed to be married. She had stretched it out way too far. She because of her past experiences knew she had to walk a tight line, if she wanted to be taken seriously about her ministry. All a woman has is her reputation, once that is torn down it is hard to rebuild, if it can be rebuilt at all. She wanted to prove that she was worthy of her calling. She learned that we really have no control over what someone says or does at another's expense.

Usually it is about envy or jealousy, like Cain, who slew his brother Abel. Why, because he was jealous of his brother's offerings (Gen 4:5-10) (KJV). The only thing we can do as Christians is walk a walk, worthy of GOD, so others can see our love for Christ.

When slander happens, we must let GOD be the vindicator. Her wanting to prove she was worthy came about because of her experience at the church on "The Other Side of Town". She had wanted to sue the church on "The Other Side of Town" as she calls it. She had gone there, new to the faith.

She had shared some very personal information about her home life with one of the Deaconess. This was to be in confidence, but all her personal business was made known to the other women in the church, plus it was all twisted around.

The women were believing she had an affair. When it was her ex-husband who had the affair. He fathered a child with his mistress. This was 3 years after they had been married. She had become a Christian during that time. The issues of her marriage drove her to find answers to all the problems happening in her life. What she came to understand was that GOD was there. His words gave her comfort and peace of mind.

She had been looking for some help or relief from the hurt. Her husband did not want to be a Christian. He loved the secular life, partying all the time. Eventually they drifted apart. In that process of drifting apart a lot of hurtful things happened. He took money out of the bank; which half was hers. He was constantly agitated with her, so there were lots of arguments. Him walking out on her a lot. Him having a baby with someone else.

She eventually had to leave the home, because he was so verbally abusive. She found herself in a shelter for women. She shared this with the Deaconess at the church on "The Other Side of Town". This made an almost impossible situation even worse, when she found out what the Deaconess had done.

She went to a Christian lawyer and yes, he informed her, she had a case, because the Churches are responsible for those, they make leaders over the congregation and how those people handle that responsibility.

A lot of the churches now are making those in Leadership roles sign a contract, about confidentiality, so they (the Churches) are not liable, but the person, who breaks that confidentiality, is liable.

After talking with a lawyer, back then, she decided not to sue, even though every part of her wanted to. He reminded her of the scripture (1Cor 6:1-11) (KJV) where one Christian is not to take another Christian before the gentile world to settle differences.

This was one of the things that led her to want to counsel women using the Bible. So, they could learn, what they are responsible for in Christ. So, they will truly help those who may be hurting and not hurt them even more. GOD also taught her about forgiveness during this time. It is like a mirror, as we want to be forgiven, we must extend forgiveness to those who have hurt us. GOD does not say we should forget, but as Christians we must forgive.

At the church on “THE OTHER SIDE OF TOWN”, the women did a lot of gossiping (some of the men too). It was awful, everything that was shared, became meat for gossip. They talked about other women if they were pretty, if they were in a financial situation, if they found anything out about the women's marriages being in disarray. They even talked about women's clothes and shoes, not being in style, they talked about the younger women, who did anything before marriage. Plus, you had better pay your tithes, then sit down and be quiet.

It was their church, they had been there a lot of years, but you had better pay those tithes, choir dues and do their programs like they wanted them to be done or they may not talk to you anymore.

It was more like a click, instead of “The older women teaching and counseling the younger women”, as in (Titus 2:1-5) (KJV). They were more interested in having their way in Church, then studying the word of GOD.

It seemed at the church on “THE OTHER SIDE OF TOWN”, most of them had forgotten the basic things like the “one another’s” in the Bible: love one another, pray one for another, forgive one another.

Courtney knew her weakness in all this, too. GOD showed her, her sinful self. When she first came into that church, she was right in that click. Oh, she wouldn't go back and share or tell what she heard. She was the other side of the coin. She was one of those who loved to hear what was being said. If one of the Deaconess or ladies in the congregation, said they would call, she made it a point to try to be home, so she could hear the latest news - (and it wasn't the GOSPEL either).

She couldn't wait for one of the Deaconess to call her, because she knew she would hear everything that was going on in the church. She could be on the phone for hours.

Them talking and her listening. Once she started going to the seminary, however, GOD convicted her of this. GOD let her know she was being a “goat”.

That is the word she heard GOD say to her one day. Courtney went into prayer right after that and asked for forgiveness about wanting to listen to the gossip.

She even stood up in Church and proclaimed to the whole church she didn't want to be a goat. She wanted to be a Sheep for GOD. So, she stopped listening and that is when the gossip really became about her.

ARE SOME OF THE CHURCHES LIKE GOATS?

Courtney read up on goats, after she heard GOD speak that word to her. Goats are ruminant animals. Like cows, they eat grass, taking in as much as they can, then later, when at rest, they bring it back up, and chew on it. They chew on it repeatedly.

Goats are stubborn too. They will buck you, resist what you want them to do, whereas sheep are gentle natured, they will follow their shepherd.

The Bible says some people in the churches are like goats, as they rebel against the word of GOD. They take it in but are never obedient to it.

They take in The Word, chew on it and chew on it, swallow it, bring it back up again, then chew on it some more, but never do what God says to do.

This is what the bible says about goats and sheep: (Matthew 25: 32-34, 41, 46) (KJV)

Goats are used to represent wickedness / sheep represent righteousness

God shall separate them one from another, as a shepherd divideth his sheep from the goats:

He shall set the sheep on his right hand, but the goats on the left.

Then shall the King say unto them on his right hand, come ye blessed of my Father, inherit the kingdom prepared for you from the foundation of the world:

glory mitz

Then shall he say also unto them on the left hand, depart from me, ye cursed, into everlasting fire, prepared for the devil and his angels

And these shall go away into everlasting punishment: but the righteous into life eternal.

GOD's Little Chapel on the Hill

The Chapel on the Hill, as it was called most of the time, was out in the country part of North Carolina, not too far from the big city of Raleigh. The highway was very picturesque, lined with trees and lots of bushes, that lead to the Church. There were two gas stations along the way. One was more a roadside stop. You could buy flowers, little odds and ends and get gas too. Two miles farther up the road was a more up to date gas station, that was forever busy.

After that, the road continued up a slight hill. On the right-hand side of the road, sitting back about half an acre away, there it was. A medium sized Chapel, that resembled a log cabin, somewhat.

The chapel was on the right. It appeared that it might hold about 300 people comfortably. Along the left side of the Chapel, was attached a long building. It had lots of windows. You could tell that these were offices. Then that building made a right turn and it looked like a banquet hall was there.

The Church looks different now, then when Courtney first joined. As you walked in the door of the Chapel now, the carpet is a light blue and all the walls are a silky, very bright white.

The pews all white, with painted little flowers and bells, along the top of the back. All the windows are frosted a light white. There were 3 along the right wall, with 3 along the left wall. Each window has a couple of words written on it, now, like in 3D. They came from (GAL 5:22) (KJV) the Fruit of the Spirit respectively: love and joy on one window, peace and long suffering on another window. With gentleness, goodness, faith, meekness, and temperance, spread out over the other windows.

During Church service, when the sun is up high, those words appear to shimmer or flicker. It is lovely. You have the feeling that the Chapel is truly anointed with the presence of GOD. The Baptismal pool was always in front of the Pulpit. No one would ever know it was there, as the communion table sat right over it. When it was open, there where stairs leading down into the pool, with stairs leading out of the pool, so you could see the people going down, then coming up again.

On the back wall, behind the choir stand, were painted two very faint images of angels, they were facing each other and blowing their trumpets. The images were painted in a very light blue. The lights in the chapel were very bright and clear, only dimmed during prayer.

They have one large TV screen in the chapel, that sits up high on the right, so the people in the back could see the announcements for that day and words to any songs, being song.

Courtney had in time, come up with the ideas of adding the frosted windows to the Chapel, the very large TV and the Christian Walk path. The TV would play Christian songs in the chapel, early on Sunday mornings, people could just come in, sit down and listen to the songs, if they wanted to. There are all types of Christian hymns and songs played, as long as, they glorified GOD. Courtney thought about how much she loved this church. She had loved this church, for a long time and always would.

THE "CHRISTIAN WALK" PATH

On the outside of the Church, they had set up a walking path. It went around the whole property, so it was a good long walk. Anyone could come and Walk the Path. Courtney had name it "The Christian Walk", because along the way were stands with scriptures, that were inside glass and metal cases. People could stop and read the scriptures, if they wanted to. Every so often the scriptures were changed.

There was a twenty-five-cent tithing bowl to enter. Of course, people didn't have to give the twenty-five cents, but there was a sign to let them know that it helped in the upkeep of the walking path.

Farther down the path was an overhead sprinkler. On hot days it came on periodically. A little passed that was scripture that talk about being Baptized and going under the water. She had worked hard to get this set up. The congregation wasn't too happy about it when she first brought it up. They went back and forth on this. They would always complain about money, like they didn't have faith that GOD would handle it. She did use the money she got in one of those anonymous envelopes, to help foot most of the cost. Now, some years later everyone was enjoying, this tree line path. She always wondered where those envelopes came from. She thought of Aaron but could not prove that he was the one sending them.

On the other side of the Christian Walk path were three old houses.

One was for the Pastor and his wife. The other two (much smaller in size) were for the associate pastors and their families if they wanted to live there. Sometimes these were used for guest visitors. Courtney lived in one of the houses, now. They were spaced far enough apart to give each family some privacy.

She was glad there was a house with the church. A few of her friends had spent a large amount of their money on building homes, when all she had to do mostly was live there. It didn't cost the church a lot to pay her salary since she lived on their property.

Directly, behind the Chapel was an open building with a roof and cement patio. The Church gave small concerts there and cookouts. She found as one of the associate pastors she didn't have to worry about money, she really was able to concentrate on the church, doctrines, getting people saved and discipled. It was a nice place to live. In the past, she had been looking forward to the day when she and Aaron would be married to each other and living there.

THE CONGREGATION!

Courtney loved to observe the new people, who entered the Church. They all, every one of them, would come in with great expectations (that great hope). (Genesis 3:15) (KJV).

Whatever the problem, somehow, they knew this was the place where they could find rest. Find an answer to their question. Find grace for whatever the problem was. (She thought of how the church was GOD's hospital to the world.)

She had been to at least 3 other churches before coming to this one. A friend from work invited her here. She was so glad she came. Each of the churches in some respects were the same. They all had the programs, the singing, announcements, prayers and of course, the sermons too. In a couple, it all seemed about the process, not as much about GOD. It was about who is going to read this and pray that. Some Sundays it seemed the church services seemed empty and not full of the Spirit.

She began to wonder if a lot of times we are doing all this in our ability and not of GOD.

At one of the churches it became about the people, who had money or status in the world. Those were the ones who decided, who did what. When it should have been about letting the Holy Spirit, lead and guide. Unfortunately, they were leaving GOD out. They knew this, but she believed, they didn't know how to get back to that correct place. They were so use to handling things themselves, instead of trusting in God. She wanted once or twice just to holler out, read the Book of Acts!

It is the Holy Spirit who established his church on the day of Pentecost. Now it seems like the churches want to function without him. If someone shouts, it is barely tolerated. If someone wants to give a testimony, it too is looked on as inconvenient. It takes too long; the program is only for 1½ hours. So, the Holy Spirit let's some churches become dry bones: not many saved, no young people baptized.

This Church here on the hill, was awesome. There was love here. There was kindness, too. She fell in love with the pastor's preaching, the people, the church itself. She knew in her heart this is where she belonged. She didn't know that GOD would make her Interim Pastor one day. That was not even a thought for her. All she wanted to do was share (teach) what had been taught to her.

There had been some challenges like with the "Christian Walk" project, and even with her and Aaron. Some in the church wanted him to marry someone else. GOD taught her, we don't know the culture of a church, at first. Just like we don't know a person's heart. There are always tares in with the wheat. The true disciples of GOD are mixed in with those that are just church goers.

It is still evident, that GOD does the calling. That the Church is the ecclesia: The called-out ones.

When people come in, they come in nervous, not knowing what they will face, but they still show up. Like a fish out of water, they have been pulled from the sea, into the wonderful Kingdom Of GOD.

Some unfortunately never come back. They don't heed the call, as they are too full of the world's system. Some are afraid of what they think they will lose. Some afraid of what they will find.

Some like Courtney when she first came into the Church, thought all who were there were righteous. Time and GOD showed her that all are there seeking: some for GOD, some for power, some for money, some for relationships, some for position.

She learned that no matter the culture, to be in GOD's will and Kingdom is still the most important thing. We must keep on searching for that right church until we find it, as she was led to this church, while she was building a relationship with The Father.

For this reason, she knew she must always preach Christ Jesus and him only. She also knew that no matter the situation we must always show love one to another, because we don't know the workings of GOD. The only way we can get a glimpse of a true believer is by the fruit they bare.

Like Pastor Paul Keys and Elder Hightown.

PASTOR KEYS AND ELDER HIGHTOWN

Pastor Paul Keys and Elder Michael Hightown were wonderful. They were always about helping others. They spent long hours on the telephones talking to those who were hurting.

Counseling the youth, those who were new to the Faith, as well as, those who were being oppressed by Satan.

There were several other Elders there, but they didn't appear to be as involved in the communities of the Church and outside the church as Elder Hightown. He would visit the nursing homes and at least a couple of times a year, the Men's prisons. Elder Hightown seemed to be a perfect fit for Pastor Keys. Whatever Pastor could not do, Elder Hightown stepped in to do.

After being at the church for several years, Courtney noticed that Pastor Keys was slowing down. It seemed what he wanted to do most now, was speaking engagements.

To Courtney, Elder Hightown could step right in for Pastor Keys at any moment, but everyone at the church thought Aaron would be the next Pastor.

Pastor Keys seemed to be training him for that position. Everyone could see Aaron's anointing, they loved to hear him preach.

Elder Hightown was the one who laid hands on Courtney. She had been going through a few awful battles. Personal battles, with her ex-husband. He had taken her money and she couldn't get it back. Emotionally hurt from the church situation at "the Church on the other side of town". The struggle with her foster mother, saying awful things to her. Her struggle wanting to teach, to do women's ministries. Even though she had been trained at the seminary, no one wanted to acknowledge that and let her teach.

Elder Hightown saw her struggle. He brought this up to her, about how he felt she was being oppressed. He then laid hands on her head, prayed a mighty prayer of release for her.

She felt he was kind of like what Boise was to Naomi. A Kinsmen Redeemer!

She began to understand the power of "Laying on of Hands", too. To have that person stand in the gap for you. To help fight the battle for you. She had heard commentaries on this from some great bible leaders, from the teachers at the school, now from one of her own church leaders, Elder Hightown.

This is what the LORD teaches about the "Laying on of Hands":

It is Doctrine.

The LAYING ON OF HANDS GIVES: (all from KJV)

Blessings and A Name (Genesis 48)

Healing (Mark 5:23)

Holy Spirit (Acts 8:18)

To Equip a person... i.e. Spiritual Authority (Acts 13:3)

We all need that Kinsman redeemer as Boise was for Naomi, in the Book of Ruth.

Not only was Ruth blessed for her commitment to Naomi, but Naomi was returned to a right standing before GOD. She who was a child of GOD, being oppressed by Satan, had lost her husband and both of her sons.

A widow in a pagan & foreign land. Poor and alone. She had a Kinsman back in her country. GOD used Ruth to make that connection for Naomi, (so she could be blessed by her kinsman). She had someone who had Power & Authority, to help fight for her, it was Boise.

Elder Hightown was that for Courtney. His power and authority were due to his Faith. So, he wasn't her family in the physical or natural world, but she knew he was in the Spiritual world.

Queen Esther Reynolds

The day that Queen walked into the Church, had been the coldest day ever recorded, for the month of May, in North Carolina. The temperature was freezing, as if it was early to mid-January.

As usual, they (her and Aaron) were standing at the door greeting the parishioners and new visitors. Then SHE walked in. Time seemed to have stopped! Courtney could remember that moment when Queen opened that door. That cold wind blowing in. Queen's long, light brown hair blowing all around. She was a beautiful black woman. She looked Ma lotto, tall, thin, her eyes were a very light purplish blue. They seemed to look right pass Courtney and landed right on Aaron.

It was always that way, from that time on. Queen's eyes were fixed on Aaron. Somehow, she always ended up close to him. Always near him. Shaking his hand, asking him questions, telling him how good his sermons were.

Courtney could see it. Aaron knew it. Temptation had come his way. Heck, the whole church could see it. He was gracious, always turning his back to Queen, never making any real eye contact, but she wanted his attention. It was apparent, to all who observed her.

From time to time Courtney would look up and around, Queen would be studying her, too. As if, to say, why you? Your pretty, but I am beautiful, or maybe she was looking for weakness in Courtney.

Courtney never faltered, she spoke to Queen kindly, always about church, women's ministries and GOD. Courtney knew very well what she was up against, but she also knew very well that her GOD was Sovereign, always in control. She also believed in Aaron. Not that his love or caring for her was all that great, but like her, his love for GOD was unshakable.

He was in love with GOD, more than he was in love with her. It was a good fit for them both because he knew she was in love with GOD more than she was in love with him. At least that is what she thought.

In her heart, she felt that was what was holding them together. The love they each had for the Father.

The tenderest moments they had as a couple were when they were sitting before a warm fireplace on a cold night. She and Aaron talking about scripture, the love of GOD, about GOD's people, and how things would be when they would be married. None of his friends could believe it, nor hers. They had taken a vow to wait for marriage and they had not crossed that line.

They talked of marriage. family, food, cooking, cars, as Aaron loved old cars. They talked mostly about the work of the Kingdom, more than anything. They could talk for hours on doctrines and revelation of the word. She wanted a small church; he wanted a bigger church. He wanted to call his "GOD's Blue Chapel", she wanted to call hers just "The Chapel". They both wanted it to show some connection to Pastor Key's Chapel. They each would just laugh and laugh, about that, as they knew they would work it out.

They had made a vow before GOD to wait and now here was Queen Esther Reynolds. Beautiful in the face, the long light brown hair (and yes, with natural highlights).

Those eyes very light purplish-blue. Who had ever seen, a black woman with extremely, light purplish-blue eyes? Blue-OK, green maybe, grey even, but not this light purplish-blue. Back then, Courtney became agitated every time she thought of this woman, chasing after Aaron, in church. In front of the whole congregation, at that.

Those eyes to Courtney were like ice: cold, with no expression. Courtney saw the look Queen gave Aaron: that long stare, that half smile, with her head tilted slightly. All Courtney could do was pray to GOD to keep Aaron strong. Time was getting close, a couple of months more and they would start putting their wedding plans in action. Courtney was under a lot of pressure at that time, while working in the ministry.

The church had made her one of the ministers and her responsibilities had increased a lot, visiting the sick and shut in, presiding at the early morning services. If needing to, still helping greet the visitors. She remembered how she and Aaron had the same Sunday's to greet the congregation. That time they spent working together drew them even closer to each other.

Plus, she had the responsibility of meeting with the Deaconess' to help them plan their programs, so that their programs were scripture based.

She also, was setting up and getting women involved in women's ministry. She knew she didn't have as much time for Aaron, as she should have. Now Queen Esther Reynolds was on the scene, and on the make for her future husband.

WHAT'S IN THE HEART WILL COME FORTH

Courtney could see that Aaron was being pulled in by Queen, little by little.

She walked into the church foyer, one Sunday, after church and there stood Queen looking up at Aaron. He went to get some information out of the car for Courtney, for the class, taking place after church. It was taking him a long time to get back, so she went to help him. There they stood, talking. They didn't stop talking either. For him, he was trying to act as though it was just casual conversation, because he reached out to place his arm around Courtney, but both he and Courtney knew, Queen wanted Aaron's attention.

Courtney was to teach a session on women and prayer. Women in the church still believe it was the men who were to pray, but she needed to teach them, that GOD wants all of us to pray.

We know this because the Bible tells us, to pray "one for another". (James 5:16) (KJV). Also, Paul says that we as Christians should pray without ceasing.

Some Christians are called to be powerful intercessors, but if they are not taught to step into their gifts, they will not push forward to do what GOD has called them to do.

All of us are called to be intercessors for others, as stated before. We are to pray for others, but GOD has given some by the power of the Holy Spirit to be intercessors extraordinaire. With their gift, they have the power to tear down strong holds, on the church and in people lives, but a lot of the gifts are not being cultivated as they should.

Not understanding we have our own gifts, talents and skills, some Christians tend to be in competition with others. We do this when we don't know who we are in Christ and are focused on someone else's gift and not our own.

We all are gifted, and each should try to learn what our gifts are, so we can step into them, bless the church, and the Kingdom. 1 Cor 12:7(KJV).

Courtney was a little upset as she needed to get this Prayer class started. She didn't want anyone in the classroom to leave.

She couldn't believe that Aaron was just taking his time getting back, as he understood the importance of the class that was about to be taught. So, Courtney went to see what was taking Aaron so long to get back, and there they stood.

Yes, Queen was on the make, it was for Aaron only, and here stood Queen and Aaron, just chatting away. Courtney could see that Aaron was being pulled in by those "icy blue" eyes!

THE CONFRONTATION

Queen wanted Aaron Flowers! She didn't care who knew it either. Who would stop her, surely not Courtney? Queen had stated to others in the Church, that all Courtney cared about was that Women's ministry program. As if, it was really going to help someone.

Courtney knew it was inevitable. The Bible says that, what is in the heart will eventually come forth. It never failed. If there was someone who resented another person's gift from GOD, that resentment would bear fruit. They would say that they couldn't stand being around that person. That, the person was trying to show off, or isn't humble enough. Not realizing that their gift is for the uplifting of the whole church, and the person with the gift needs to bring it forward to glorify GOD.

Sometimes this resentment happened because a person feels superior in intellect or holds a high position in the world or if they had more money than others. It would bear fruit. They would want the best seats in the church or hold the most important positions. What happened in Church had to go through them. They would have to handle it. The people with less money or status, would sit in the back and be quiet.

Courtney tried not to let what was building in her heart towards Queen get out of hand, but she knew it was inevitable.

Courtney wanted to talk with Queen about her actions towards Aaron. She wanted to call it a conversation but knowing Queen it would be more of a confrontation, than a conversation. Everything was a fight for Queen, especially, if it was not her way. So, a confrontation was going to happen, either Queen's way, with everyone looking on and it being out of control, (probably just the way Queen would want it to be). That would show everyone she was superior, smarter than Courtney. Courtney wanted it to be her way, where it would be under control, just her and Queen. So, the inevitable happened, Courtney asked for a "meeting" with Queen.

The pressures of life, the working out of Satan's ills on all GOD's creatures is a hard thing. Courtney was feeling blessed to be a child of GOD. Not that things didn't happen to them, but she knew as a Child of GOD, she was under the protection of the Father, by the Shed Blood of his only begotten Son, Our Lord and Savior Jesus Christ.

The moment Queen walked into Courtney's office; Courtney knew Queen's claws were out. Queen threw her purse in the chair, that stood in front of Courtney's desk. She leaned forward, placed her hands on the desk, and looked straight at Courtney with those icy purplish-blue eyes, not blinking once.

Courtney slowly stood up, walked to the right side of her desk. She very slowly said "Queen, I know, you know, this is about Aaron. He is a nice-looking man and a very nice man. I also know, you have been through somethings and have been hurt. I see you talking to Aaron an awful lot.

Um, I just wanted to let you know in case you aren't sure, or didn't know, but Aaron and I are going to be married."

"You are one of the best-looking women in the church, you have money, but if you had attended one of my session you would know, GOD is the one who decides who is to be married and who we should marry.

I would like for you to back off from wanting to get attention from Aaron. You talk to him about kids, cars, you are always asking him questions. I am personally asking for a little more respect for him (him being a Reverend) and for me also."

Queen stood up straight, looked up in the air, did a 45 degree turn towards Courtney and said "Look I am not into all this Biblical counseling stuff. I know how I feel. I believe I know what Aaron is feeling too. FRUSTRATED... I'm sure, trying to wait on you, to make up your mind, on whether you want him or GOD. I haven't seen anything saying you two are getting married, only heard, that you are friends and not even committed to each other. Yes, I have money. I think I can help him get to where he needs to be and give him what he needs. If I can, I will make him mine!"

Courtney replied," Your walking in the natural and not in the Spirit of Christ. You haven't a clue about what's really important to him. Queen, GOD is not going to bless this, you know that."

Queen ended the conversation by saying "and what are you walking in, Miss Thang? Your jealous because he may just want me and not you." She picked up her purse, walked to the door. She looked back over her shoulder and said, "You and your oh so righteous self." Courtney fell back in her chair, overwhelmed by this woman's anger.

It always amazed Courtney, as to how we as women can dislike someone, not because they have done anything to us, but because their hair is longer, their complexion is lighter. They are taller, skinner and sometimes like this instance, Queen was jealous over what Courtney had with Aaron and her knowledge of God's Word. Courtney thought of Cain and Abel. How Cain slew his brother, because his brother's offerings to GOD, were preferred to his own. (Genesis 4:113) (KJV). When Cain could have offered the same type of offering as Abel but wouldn't. Queen could take the time to look for someone, who could really like and love her, but she wanted to destroy what Courtney had with Aaron.

She wanted him for herself, even though he didn't belong to her. Courtney knew she needed to be in prayer, a lot now. She needed to read back through her own notes on prayer.

Courtney also understood Queen more than Queen realized, this is what she went to seminary for. To counsel women biblically, those who were hurting and lost in their direction on what GOD wanted them to do. She thought she could even like Queen, a lot as a Christian friend, if Queen could just come in line with the word of GOD and not walk around angry all the time. Queen needed to stop trying to control everything with her money, and let GOD be GOD. Let him do the work, the way he wanted to.

Courtney remembered her own hurt, when the man she loved became involved with someone else. How he took her money out of the bank. She had heard that Queen had lost a lot of money to her ex-husband due to their divorce. Courtney's mind quickly went back to the matter at hand.

She thought. Aaron belongs with me. What Queen didn't know, and what Courtney remembered, as she was sitting there, was that Aaron had and always would belong to GOD, first.

AARON ON THE ROCKY ROAD

Each of the ministers had a weekend to be on call, on the Encouragement telephone lines. To help a sister or brother with any Christian questions.

Usually, Friday's were very busy. People would call from mid-day, well into the evening.

This was a special service offered after they (the congregation) had attended several mandatory classes. The classes were on Prayer, Finances, Marriage, being Single, Evangelizing and several others as well. They had to go through all these foundational classes.

Then, if they still had concerns, they could call the ministers, to talk about any issues they were still having. The calls were logged in and recorded.

They were to last no more than 10 or 15 minutes. If more counseling was needed, they could then sign up for the group meetings held by the ministers. If that didn't help, then and only then, did they get to be counseled by Pastor Keys.

This call came in about 6:30pm Eastern time on Friday. It was almost time for the phones to go offline. The ministers came on at 12n and went off at 7pm. The call logged was from Queen Esther Reynolds and Reverend Aaron Flowers was working the phones. A couple of the other ministers had taken the earlier shifts. Apparently, she was needing help with her car. Queen's car had broken down in a not so nice an area. Queen knew Aaron loved cars, studied on them in his spare time. That was the hook. Aaron went to help Queen.

Aaron knowing Queen and what she was up to, always wanting to get attention from him, he called Elder Hightown. He left Elder a message to let him know, Queen had called the church's Encouragement line pleading for help.

Her car had broken down on Highway 46, not a good area for a woman to be in alone and she had her son with her. Aaron was on his way to where she was, to help her get home. He asked Elder Hightown to meet him on Highway 46, near the Big Cup Coffee Shop.

Aaron felt he knew himself, well. Oh, before he was saved, even early on, his issue was always with women. They were always on him, always chasing him. They were always in his face, smiling at him, trying to talk with him, cooking for him, buying him clothes, sending him flowers, cards, etc. He knew his looks had a lot to do with this. Their first comment would be," you have the longest eyelashes I have ever seen on a man. Your eyes are gorgeous."

He had to learn to overcome his ego, his Pride. He learned to keep his mind on Jesus. He was so thankful that GOD called him. Before giving his life to Christ, he had a lot of drama with women, all his young adult life. It had costed him money, time and a lot of himself, by always trying to make them happy.

He felt he would be OK in this situation going to help Queen, because no matter what she did, he loved GOD, he loved Courtney. As a precaution, he asked Elder Hightown to meet him there.

Aaron noticed Queen had all these shopping bags in the back seat of her car. Lost in the maze of all those bags, was little Ricky. A beautiful little boy, quiet, but pleasant. Aaron thought to himself, he would one day like to have a kid like little Ricky. He looked at Queen, she had it all together, money, looks, those purplish-blue eyes. She could have any man she wanted, why was she on him so hard. He had hoped as he had talked more about Courtney, to her, she would get the hint and move her attention elsewhere. The word was she had lived with her ex-husband about 6 years before they got married. Once they were married, it lasted all of 18 months. He thought," what could have been the issue with them?"

He prayed for Queen at that moment.

She appeared very independent, but there seemed to be a real neediness about her. The thought, came to him," she could overwhelm a man with always being so needy. Everything would always be about her."

He thought of the class Courtney taught on contentment, then he laughed to himself. Thinking, "Queen really needs that class."

Aaron knew he and Courtney had a good thing. He had a bright future ahead with Courtney. Church ministry and them traveling for Christ. He was so excited about all that was ahead for them. He was going to put a little pressure on Courtney to go ahead and at least set the wedding date. It was time. He realized he had someone who loved the LORD with the same intensity he did, and it wasn't about money, or control. It was about GOD.

WHAT HAPPENED TO ELDER HIGHTOWN

Aaron and Queen sat there almost an hour, but no Elder Hightown. Aaron checked the car; he knew the engine had conked out. Why it had, he wasn't sure of, but he knew it was the engine. They waited for Elder Hightown. No returned calls, no answering his phone. Aaron could see that little Ricky was tired. He had fallen asleep back there in his car seat. Aaron agreed to take Queen home.

When he got her home, he took Ricky into his arms, with about 5 of those big bags. Queen had her purse and about 5 more bags. They entered her apartment; it was extremely nice: big, clean, nice picture window. She took a few of the bags into her bedroom, then she came and got little Ricky.

She told Aaron, she wanted to give him something for his time and travel. He told her no, but she insisted, then she stated, he could give it to the church, if he liked.

When she came out of the bedroom, she had changed into a very lovely peach dress, that clung to her slightly. She smelled differently too. He stood there, not able to move, not able to really look at her either. She handed him the envelope with cash inside.

She came closer to him, then leaned in to plant a kiss on his cheek. She said, “thanks for helping me.” Then she kissed him on the lips lightly. It was suddenly like a movie where he was watching himself. He was shocked back to reality, when he looked at her. All he could see were those eyes, but they weren't soft. It was as if they were penetrating right into his sole. Those cold purplish-blue eyes. He fell back up against the door. He regained his composure and apologized.

Queen said.” Aaron what's wrong? You know you enjoyed that kiss. I know I did. Aaron, I would be good for you and your ministry. People automatically gravitate to me. I could help you go far with your ministry. I do have some pull in the community.

Aaron said," I'm sorry, I love Courtney. I can't do this." Queen replied quickly, "She can't help you. All she has is her teaching and wanting to preach. You love the church. I love the church and all the programs." He said, "No, I have to leave now. Please forgive me. I should have stopped this long ago." He could hear her saying, "Aaron you love the Church, I love the Church."

Right then he heard the Holy Spirit say to him, "but does she love GOD the Father?" Aaron knew he had to get away from there quickly.

As he was driving home, his mind was racing, going over that scene that had just happened. He thought of Courtney. What would his little episode with Queen do to her heart. He knew Queen would let it be known that she kissed him, especially if he tried to ignore her now. He knew her well enough to know that she would try to hurt Courtney, just to get back at him. She would hurt Courtney in an instant without even batting those "cold blues" as Courtney would say. He knew he needed to talk with Elder Hightown or Pastor. No! It had to be Elder.

Pastor Keys! Aaron thought; Oh no. Pastor Keys had a lot of confidence in him, as did Courtney. What would he say to them? The Church! What would they think? He took his hand and hit the steering wheel! The more he thought about what happened, the more he realized this could be ugly. Courtney is to be ordained in just a couple of days. He thought to himself "Aaron what were you thinking? That you were invincible to women and their charms. What point was I trying to make? That I could handle any situation like this one, now?"

He knew he should have prayed more. Everything could be in shambles just because of this one little incident. Hurting Courtney, disappointing Pastor Keys, having to explain it all to Elder Hightown. He prayed out loud, "Father forgive me my over confidence, my weakness." He needed space, that was the answer, he needed to be off the scene for a while. Just a few days, until Courtney was ordained, then they could talk about the scene with Queen, in detail.

He thought of a solution. He was going to go visit his friend (Timothy Evenstal) in California. He had told his friend (Timothy) he would be there to hang out with him before he got married.

Timothy was a Pastor of a small church in Oakdale, California. Timothy could also counsel him about this situation and why he let himself be pulled in by Queen. He knew this wasn't Queen's fault, but mostly his.

This was the perfect time for him to go. He could catch an early morning flight out to California. He raced home, called the airport to check on flights going out the next morning. If he was at the airport by 6am, he could get the 8am eastern flight that connected through Texas then to California. He packed a light bag of clothing, then headed to the airport. He would just hang out there until he was able to board his flight.

In the meantime, he needed to talk to Elder Hightown, as his mind was still racing, wildly for an answer.

He needed to step back, get away for a while. Away from those images in his mind, of Queen and those cold blue eyes. Away from the reality of hurting Courtney. He could not bear to see her cry now. This was to be a happy time for her, a joyous time. She had been waiting a few years to get to this point. This was a pivotal moment in her life, to be an ordained minister.

Her not trying to please man but being obedient to GOD. He needed Elder Hightown to keep Queen busy, away from Courtney, until Sunday service was over, and Courtney had been ordained.

ELDER HIGHTOWN

He seemed to fully understand his calling. He was a Deacon of the church. He knew he was there to protect. There to help heal, help watch over the flock. To lay hands on those being oppressed, to pray for those in need.

It was clear, Elder Hightown, loved GOD dearly.

He loved his calling. He would step in, pray and preach the word if that was necessary. He walked in the Power and Authority that was given to him by Jesus Christ. Courtney had heard him say more than once, that all who have been called (basically the whole church, the ecclesia) "The Called-Out Ones," have been given power and authority, but most of us seem to forget that. It seems to Courtney, that Elder Hightown never forgot his calling. Seems like he and Pastor Keys lived only to due the will of GOD.

Pastor Paul Keys, a good family man was always on the go, except for Sunday's. He would make it back to be in the pulpit, every Sunday. When he couldn't and if the other ministers couldn't, Elder Hightown would step in.

This only happened once or twice, since Courtney had been there. Once was during a bad snowstorm, that happened suddenly up North. Pastor had travel up North to do a convention and a few of the other ministers with him, their flights were delayed.

Aaron had to work, so Elder stepped right in, he made sure the church was open for those who felt they needed to come. That was Elder Hightown, never missing a beat for The Lord.

He had laid hands on Courtney. She had gotten to know him as he was visiting the nursing home were her foster mother was. Even though they attended the same church, they never really had any real conversations, until she saw him as the nursing home. He would listen to the seniors and pray for them. That is how it came about him laying hands on her. She told him about the different situations, that had occurred in her life. He informed her, he thought she had evil forces coming up against her. He wanted to lay hands on her, pray for her. So, he did.

Elder was a short, stout man, with grey and black, shiny hair. Even though he was older, he looked strong, and no doubt he had a strong will. He was on his second marriage. He had lost his first wife and baby, years ago to the flu.

Mary, his second wife, was a little younger than him. She seemed to be the perfect person for him. She was always baking cookies, any kind. She would bring them to the church, give them out to whomever might want any. Elder stated that is why he fell in love with her. He went to pick her up for their first date. When he walked into her house, the smell of cookies baking, made him think of his childhood, as his mom baked a lot too.

She had baked, earlier that day, some chocolate chip cookies from scratch with macadamia nuts in them. She gave him a couple of bags and he thought they were marvelous. He stated, he knew then, that he was going to marry her. Mary had never been married, had always been in church and had such a nice personality. She loved to sing with the choir. Courtney loved them both. They were a beautiful couple, always upbeat, working together for the Lord. They were more like her family now. They were her family.

Aaron's call to Elder

Aaron was finally able to get through to Elder Hightown. He and his wife were just about to leave the hospital. They were at the hospital pharmacy, picking up the prescription for Mary.

Aaron's first words to Elder were, "Michael, I have been calling you all evening! Where are you? Man, have I messed up? I took Queen home and." Elder cut in and said: "Aaron, oh no, now come on, nothing happened right? We talked about Queen and this scenario. Queen wants to use her money to control things.

We have been through this, she even wanted to control the Women's Ministry. Offering to give a large amount of money to it, if she could say who was in charge and the subjects that would be taught. If Courtney knew that she would be devastated. Thank goodness Pastor Keys, does not look at the money a person has but the anointing from the Holy Spirit."

Aaron shot back; "I know, I know. I was too confident in myself. I got myself together before it went too far, but the situation was not good. She kissed me, a light kiss and I let her. Elder when I opened my eyes, she had been looking at me the whole time. She had never closed her eyes. She was sizing me up."

Elder stated." OK so what now? How can I help you?" Aaron replied." First thing in the morning, I will fly out to California. I just need to get off the scene for a little while, until Courtney is ordained, and Queen sees she don't have any power in this situation. Then when I come back, I will meet with Pastor Keys and then Courtney. I want Courtney and I to go ahead and set a wedding date." Elder stated." You know this is going to hurt Courtney. You not being there for her ordination and that's not even saying anything about that kiss."

Aaron said,' I know, but I think it's best right now. It wasn't a real kiss, but it is the fact I did take her home after her car broke down. I was in her apartment, and then this so-called kiss.

The more I thought about it, the more I realized this could look bad to the church folks. I need to just step away for a while. I've called my job. They know I have an emergency and that I need to fly out to California. I can work from there, also.

Second item. Is there anything you can do to keep Queen from talking to Courtney about this or can you talk to Courtney, explain what happened? I'll drop a message into Courtney's voice mail, letting her know I am sorry and that I love her."

Elder in a low tone said," OK Aaron, I will see what I can do, but I do wish you would be there on Sunday for Courtney." Aaron said," I wish I could, too."

Elder's call to Courtney

Elder Hightown called Courtney, first to confirm that Aaron was OK. He then, very easily explained that it appeared, Aaron wouldn't be able to make her ordination. She kept asking him why? What could have happened that would stop him from being there?

Elder Hightown said one word. “Queen." The phone was silent for a very long time. He called her name once, "Courtney?" Then again "Courtney are you there?" Finally, she said, "I’m here Elder. What happened between Aaron and Queen?" Elder explained that Queen was OK, as was Aaron.

Elder Hightown went on to explain how Queen had called the Encouragement Line needing help and Aaron went to help her. Elder quickly added. “He called me before he left church, asking that I meet them on highway 46.”

He explained, “I didn't get the call until much later, as I had taken Mary to the emergency room. She had a tooth that had abscessed. By the time, I got back to him, the damage had been done already.”

Courtney responded with a very slow response. “Damage, what damage?” He said "Yes. Damage." He couldn't see it, but tears had swelled in her eyes, she didn't even know until one dropped on her hand and ran down her fingers. Elder could hear a little tension in her voice, so he went on to explain what Aaron had told him about the situation.

He informed her, he didn't want Aaron to leave town, but Aaron had made up his mind, about leaving town even before they had spoken. Aaron was, on his way to the airport. He told her that Aaron would call her just before his flight took off. Elder stated, he would be over, and Mary would be with him. They arrived 45 minutes later at her home. It was such a peaceful place just behind the church. A nice path to walk along.

The house was small and cozy, but never the smell of cookies baking, just the faint scent of flowers, always flowers.

Courtney was sitting on the front porch, looking very solemn faced. She had a very beautiful shawl around her shoulders. Blue and white which were her favorite colors.

She was a very nice-looking young lady in her own right. Too bad about how Queen wanted to just mess things up for her. Courtney's life had not been easy, either. He thought about how Satan, uses people, to try to hurt the Children of GOD.

Mary sat down beside Courtney. She hugged Mary, gently. Courtney asked how she was doing. Mary stated that her face still felt unreal, as it was still swollen a lot. She had taken some antibiotics, plus a Motrin for pain. So, she was good for the night.

Courtney stood up and said "let's go in the house, get out of the night air. Hey, you could stay here with me tonight, then get up early in the morning to go home". Elder agreed.

It was a long night for Elder Hightown and Courtney. Mary went to bed, shortly after getting there, but Elder and Courtney talked way into the morning hours. They were both glad they didn't have to get up very early in the morning. Elder knew he would have to go see Queen. He had a plan of what he would ask her to do, since she had brought all this into action. He was glad they were at Courtney's house. That way, Courtney could look after Mary, when he went to go see Queen. He would know where everyone was.

Elder Hightown Visits Queen

Queen didn't really want to talk with him, when he called her, but he let her know it was about Aaron. Never really saying what it was about, then she stated it was OK for him to come over to visit her. She had a beautiful apartment on the best side of town. He asked her about her car.

She stated, it had been picked up by her mechanic and to his surprise, she also stated he (her mechanic) was upset with her, because he had asked her not to drive that car. Apparently, it needed some engine work. She had another, newer car, but for some reason had decided to drive the older one. Elder thought to himself." Oh, I know the reason Queen. You wanted Aaron's attention."

Elder never let her know he knew what really happened the night before, just that Aaron had to go out of town on an emergency. This had happened before, so it wasn't a shock to anyone. Elder did tell Queen; Aaron had made him aware of her car troubles and ask that he check on her.

He then stated, he wanted her to participate in Sunday's Service. Aaron was called out of town unexpectedly and a couple of the other ministers were traveling too. He told her he needed her to Host the program.

Her first statement was, “Isn’t Courtney being ordained?” To which he responded, “Yes”, and that he needed her (Queen to step in for Aaron). It was important to the Church, that they had continuity before the congregation. He explained to her, about Mary being at the hospital on Friday night and him now needing to be sure he could take her back to the hospital at any moment, if anything came up.

He had with him just what he needed her to do and before he left, she had said yes. He was praying as he walked back to his car, that this would work out OK. He had read these verses from the bible to Queen, before he left: 5 This then is the message which we have heard of him (GOD), and declare unto you, That GOD is Light, and in him is no darkness at all. 6 If, we say that we have fellowship with him and walk in darkness, we lie and do not the truth

7 But if we walk in the light, as he is in the light, we have fellowship one with another, and the blood of Jesus Christ, his son cleanseth us, from all sin. 1JOHN 1:5-7(KJV)

For this is the message that ye have heard from the beginning, that we should love one another. 1JOHN 3:11(KJV)

He knew he got her with the Scriptures. Her facial expression changed as she was listening to the words of GOD. Now back to Courtney, to let her know, that Queen would Host the program on tomorrow.

The program was good, Queen did a really good job of Hosting and Courtney was able to do her Sermon without any indication that anything had happen, contrary in her life.

Courtney standing before the congregation gave Queen thanks for stepping in for Aaron, who had to leave urgently. She never let Queen know that she knew what had happened on last Friday night. She had prayed on this. She knew even though, Queen had set out to hurt her, she could not let that situation cause her to sin. She (wondered in her heart) if this was a test. She prayed to the Father, that she would please pass it, if so.

When she finally arrived home that Sunday afternoon, late, she saw that Aaron had left a message saying he loved her. Asking her to forgive him for his error in judgment. He let her know he needed to spend some time alone with GOD.

He was going to stay with Timothy Evenstal and his wife for a couple of weeks. Once he was settled in, he would call her. He let her know, they would have a good long talk, which also would include discussing marriage.

The Call

Courtney smiled, with a sigh of relief. The number on her answering machine was that of Aaron Flowers. She was so excited to see it she almost didn't pick up the receiver to talk. She just wanted that moment to last forever. To be able to see his name, his number displayed on her answering machine. She had wanted numerous times over the last few weeks to call him, but Elder Hightown had asked her not to.

Elder stated that Aaron needed time. Time to sort through all that he had felt and experienced, that Friday night in Queen's apartment.

She lifted the receiver, she heard him say. “Courtney this is Aaron.” How are you?” Her heart melted! She fell back on to the soft blue couch and put her feet up on the sofa. It was almost 11am, she still had on her terry, white robe and soft white socks. She had decided to hang around the house this Saturday morning and she was now glad she did. She heard herself say “Aaron, Oh Aaron, I am OK! I have been wanting and waiting to hear from you. When are you coming home? I have missed you. Everyone at church has been asking about you and if you are OK. If your job was OK, since they know you have to travel a lot.

Oh, how is your friend Timothy and his wife?” Aaron replied “Nea! Nea slow down. Timothy, his wife and their newborn baby are fine. I have enjoyed being here with him and his family.

His wife's name is Emily and their brand-new baby girl. Cenya is beautiful. Big bright eyes. She is so soft. I was almost afraid I would hold her to tight. They have been wonderful to me!"

Aaron paused, he called her "Nea." Whenever he called her "Nea" he was extremely serious. She knew the small talk was over. "Nea". that was his nick name for her. She always wondered how he came up with Nea, but she liked it. "Yes Aaron" she replied.

He stated, "I won't be back for a while. I am still having some issues with how I let you down. How I let Queen manipulate me. You see it wasn't just you I let down. Nea, it was GOD, my Father, also. My vows to him, that is what is hurting me right now. Somehow I feel I let him down." Courtney replied "Aaron you have got to get passed this. Our Father is very forgiving you know that. We will make mistakes."

Aaron replied, "Yes, Nea, I know we will, but did it have to be in this area?" The Holy Spirit is working on me with this.

So, I need some time to work through all this before I make a commitment." She heard herself say calmly, "How much time Aaron?"

He answered "Nea, I know I hurt you. I am hurting you now, but I need time, else I will never get pass this." She smiled and stated "OK Aaron. You gave me time. Lots of time. I can do the same. I'm not angry. Aaron, I just want you to come home when you are ready. What about your job?"

Finally, he said "OH, that is the other item I need to explain. Since I am here in California. They need me to stay out here for a bit. Maybe, a couple of months. Nea I love you deeply. I do and don't you forget that. OK?"

She answered with, "OK Aaron, I'll let Elder Hightown know you called and Mary too. Have you talked with Pastor Keys? He misses you greatly." He replied "Yes, Yes, I have spoken to both. They both are aware." Inside Courtney was begging, Aaron please don't go, but on the outside, she had to reassure him all was OK.

She knew GOD was sovereign over all things. God works things out for the better of the Kingdom and for those that love him. Aaron loves the Father more than anything. Somehow with that thought, she had peace and was praying for happiness for Aaron.

The time past slowly, a call came in here and there. She even flew out to California, for a weekend, once. He lived in a very quiet, tree lined neighborhood. She had gotten a hotel room near the beach. They stayed on the beach a lot that weekend. Nothing romantic happened, no hand holding or kisses, nor any talks of them building a life together.

He was very quiet. She noticed he kept looking deeply into her eyes for long periods of time, as though he was searching for something There were lots of long walks on the beach. She met Timothy Evenstal, his wife Emily and their beautiful little girl Cenya. They had a wonderful time talking about the LORD, the Bible, the young church, children, food and of course, cars.

Timothy talked about the plans for his church and to her surprise, how Aaron was pictured in those plans.

Timothy was speaking as though Aaron would be his right-hand man in the Lord, as Elder Hightown was for Pastor Keys. Aaron would become, one of the Reverends there. Aaron never disagreed, so she knew he had planned to stay in California a long while. Back at the hotel room alone, she found herself on her knees crying, asking GOD to give her strength to continue to make it through this very difficult time.

As, she flew home she thought of how it was such a good weekend. She gave God thanks for the time she had been able to share with Aaron. She prayed he would find what he was looking for and the peace he needed. She was glad God was sovereign in all things and that she didn't have to try to do this alone.

The busier Aaron became out there with the church, with helping his friend, the less and less the calls came in.

She heard from him on holidays, she heard from him on her birthday, but they became more and more infrequent. She knew that what had happened, had been more then he could deal with at the time. He was so confident in himself, so she gave him the space he needed. Oh, she knew that he and Elder talked. He and Pastor talked, but something had changed, between him and her

Time went on. Queen moved on to another church. Pastor only did sermons occasionally. She, Elder and Mary were still there, as where a lot of the ministers. They had a couple of new Reverends. Over the years a couple of new Pastors came in and in between, she, the Ministers and the Deacons held down the fort along with Pastor Keys.

There were even a couple of other women ministers by this time, and she would always say to that "To GOD Be The Glory." She had prayed hard, worked hard to make sure women who were called into the ministry were trained and recognized, also, not just the men.

People stop asking her about Aaron. Everyone had moved on, she had to too. At least some, but occasionally, (like yesterday, while sitting in her home office) her mind drifted back to so many years ago. To that broad smile, those deep dimples and that proud walk. Those evenings sitting before the fireplace, and how he wanted to have a big church. He would name it God's Blue Chapel. How she wanted a smaller Church and wanted to name it The Chapel. She never pictured them being apart, but this thought always came to her. That we sometimes must put those things near and dear to us, the important things, on the altar for the sake of the Kingdom, as Abraham did with his son, Isaac. (Genesis 22: 1-13) KJV

Sunday Morning-back to the future!

So here she was after so many years, waiting with anticipation, her being inducted as interim Pastor.

The church and Pastor Keys had asked that she fill the role this time, just for a while, because she had worked so hard on the "Christian Walk" path.

It had been such a success for the church. As she sat there, in her usual spot, she thought she saw Aaron sitting in the very back of the church. There seem to be someone with him that looked like him also. All these years, all this time, over 25 years had gone by, 26 to be exact.

Was it her imagination or did she really see him in the congregation? She looked at Elder, who looked old now and moved slow, Mary still with him. She looked at him, then to the audience, back to him, then to the audience again. He got it. There was someone there she wanted him to see and he did. He nodded his head, yes.

THE SERMON

She had prayed over, cried over, walked the floor over and mused over her sermon.

She had wanted this one to ring in their ears and hearts for a long time. She was hoping to push all the right spiritual buttons for the Lord. She prayed she would be able to say just what God had wanted her to say at this time.

She had given many sermons before, all God inspired but because she was now the Interim Pastor, at least for a while, she wanted this one to be special. She prayed for the Holy Spirit to touch her. To anoint her for this special message and she knew he did, as she came away with 3 areas to address. Then she asked that he (The Holy Spirit) show her how to bring them all, together.

The first topic had to do with the inner and outer courts. That we as Christians get so involved in what's going on in the outer court, we tend to forget about the inner court, were God dwells.

To the entire Church:

Courtney told them we must be mindful and INTENTIONAL to remember that God has called us to dwell in the inner court with him, not just in the outer court, where we think on our problems and issues.

Where we think that our singing, marching, preaching and programs are for him, but we make them all about us. Who can pray the best, who can sing the best Who looks better than whom, in how we dress?

Jesus Christ tore down the wall of separation, between GOD and man. (the curtain was torn into, in the Holy Temple, from the top to the bottom).

We are to leave the issues of life on the altar, give it to Jesus, as he will handle it, no matter what it is. So, that we can enter the most HOLY OF HOLIES, were GOD dwells, without us thinking about the outer court, about ourselves, all the time. We go in cleaned up by the Blood of Jesus Christ, made righteous by what he did on the cross.

Courtney asked "May we stop and be quiet for just a minute or two, to give GOD magnificent worship. Not mentioning us for a change, just making this time about him and how great he is:

Blessed are you Lord GOD, King of the Universe, Creator of all things. All things are held together by your power and might. The hidden things of you are Blessed, those things we don't understand, unless you reveal them. You are intricate, faithful and pure Lord GOD, beautiful in all your ways. May your Kingdom reign now and forever more. AMEN!"

To the Deacons, Deaconesses, The Ministers, and the Reverends of the CHURCH:

She said this..."You are an example to the whole world of God's mighty power. As Lazarus was called out of the grave and as Jesus told them nearby, to remove his grave clothes, loose him.

So, we are (myself included) called out of a kind of grave, where we had to die to self and the world first.

Then, GOD calls us to come forward, just as he did to Lazarus.

I want you to understand that the power that moved Lazarus forward, is the same power that moves us forward. Can you see in your mind's eye, Lazarus hopping forward, still bond in his grave clothes)? We are examples to today's world, as Lazarus was an example to the Pharisees and Sadducees in Jesus time. Attaining to the Power of GOD.

Our churches are not preaching and teaching in and of themselves, IT IS THE POWER OF THE HOLY SPIRIT working in them. If at any time or all at once we stop preaching Christ Jesus, they will become as dry bones. Our churches would drop as a lifeless man to his knees and keel over dead. They would fall again, as men, dead to GOD.

The world is in amazement, as it sees the number of people in church each week. The world sometimes would like to remove these churches, as the Pharisees and Sadducees, wanted to plot to kill Lazarus as he sat at dinner with our LORD Jesus Christ, but they couldn't. John 12: 1-11(KJV).

Lazarus was a living example to all the people, of GOD's mighty power, because of this, the world will say it is of GOD! So, it is important for us to remember and to remind others, that we are led by the Power of GOD, The Holy Spirit. That it is not in our ability that we preach and teach the WORD OF GOD. We are Lazarus brought forth. Called by Our Lord Jesus Christ.

Finally, to the congregation she wanted to address how she wanted to conduct herself as Interim Pastor: Courtney stated it was her belief and prayer, that their church would be like a Spiritual Hospital, that could truly help heal the broken hearted, the down trodden, those who are burden by life's problems. That their main purpose as the Church was to always lead the broken to Christ Jesus. She didn't want the Church sermons to always be about money or leading up to money.

Even though the Churches need mammon to do the work that is set before them.

She didn't want to be like the Physicians in the parable of the woman with the issue of blood, (the woman being a type of the older Church) (Matt 9:20-22)(KJV) who had been to numerous Physicians and neither of them could heal her, but had taken all she had, and as a matter of fact she had been made worst.

She wanted to be like Jairus, a “type” of a Church Leader, who willing came to Jesus, fell at Jesus feet, asking for healing for his daughter. She wanted the Church leaders to come together for intercessory prayer, each Sunday for half an hour before church started, to invoke the power of the Holy Spirit.

In closing, she asked for prayer for herself, that she would be a good Shepard in leading, and a good sheep in following Jesus Christ, always, with love and humbleness of heart. Amen!

AARON AND JOSHUA

As they were pulling out of the parking lot, Aaron's son asked him “Dad why didn't you tell them or let them know you were here?” Aaron, the young man's father, reached into his jacket pocket, pulled out his white, Pastor's collar. He put it in place and with a very faraway look in his eyes he just said “NO”. “No need now. Too much time has gone by. Those old hurts have been long healed and forgiven or forgotten. Stored in deep places now. She is happy. She has her Chapel and.”

His son Joshua, quickly cut in and said “Chapel, you mean that little old church back there by the lake?” Dad you have a nice size church with over a 1000 people, some Sundays.” Aaron shot back. “Yes, her Chapel!” “She has her Chapel and her one true love. GOD.”

The atmosphere in the car was quiet now. Aaron fell into a daze of memories, he thought of the first time he saw Courtney, his heart skipped a beat, maybe two. He smiled inside at that thought. Aaron thought of how hard she was trying to help the ministers and the church understand that women are also called into the Ministry and should not be abandoned by their brothers in the Faith. Church leaders must have a program in place to help these women, to become what GOD has called them to be: Teachers, Ministers, Evangelist and in certain cases Pastors. If not, women who are untaught, in the church, or don't understand the call these women are called to, will try to stop them or maybe even destroy them.

Women can be attacked very badly by "the Martha's" of the church, when they are called into the Five-Fold ministry. It is sad, as those women have not been taught Luke 10:38-42.

It is only when a Pastor has a program already in place, to help these women, are they able to be recognized as those called into the Five-Fold ministry and able to step into their calling.

That was one of the main things he did at his church. Set up a program, to recognize women who are Teachers, Preachers, Ministers and to get them Trained. That is what he believes made his Church the success it is. Women from all over came in to be trained. He believed this was GOD's plan. He didn't understand this until many years later.

He was jolted back to reality by more of Joshua's questions. “Do you think Mom knew Dad?” Aaron answered back “Knew what Joshua?” Joshua stated, “That you loved the Pastor Lady back at that Church, many years ago.” Aaron answered “I loved your mom very much, Joshua. She was a good woman and I miss her dearly.” Joshua replied. "I know that Dad. You were good to her, to me, to your whole congregation, but she would from time to time say. I wonder sometimes what's on your Dad's mind. I know he loves me, I have a good life, but from time to time, he seems so far away. Then I see him reading his Bible and I know he has found relief, in GOD, from what might be troubling him.”

"Josh!" (that is what Aaron called his son, whenever he was about to get serious). "I never told your mom about that time in my life. I made a mistake. A small mistake in some people eyes, but to me, it went to my core. Sometimes we don't know how much we are his (God's) until we make a mistake. I knew I loved God, but it was after that little mistake, that I knew I was totally his. The Holy Spirit let me know. I found myself on my knees asking GOD to forgive me, to help me. I mourned all night long. I knew at that moment I would not wonder far from his Word again."

"I also knew I let down some wonderful people that were counting on me to be there. I know now, I was loved a lot. Back then, I was questioning if I was really loved at all. I understand now why she was so totally devoted to him" Joshua said flippantly "Him who, Dad"?

"GOD" Aaron said softly. "She loved God more than anything. She was taking a chance letting me in. She didn't want to be pulled away from him.

I almost did just that. I'm glad we have a GOD who is all knowing, all forgiving and restores all things. She was called to be an example, Joshua, to and for other women. No matter how small a thing, we may think it is, she has been true to that calling."

Joshua mumbled "She is just a little old lady now. She still looks good for her age, but what is she 60, 61 now? I think mom would look better." Aaron smiled a big smiled and said "Yes, your mother was beautiful inside and out, and a real looker too. Gorgeous. Thank goodness no icy blue eyes."

Joshua smiled and his mind drifted to other things. Suddenly, Aaron sat forward and said "Wait!!!" "I need to go back. It's not finished yet. I had hoped that all was finished this time, but that is not what my heart is saying. I need to talk to her once again. Let her know what GOD had led me to do for the Kingdom, because of her influence."

GREEN FLOWERS AND WHITE ROSES

Elder Hightown appears to the left. Then his wife, Mary walks up from the right, holding a small bouquet of green and white flowers. Aaron steps forward. Courtney is lead out of the house to an open patio. In the background is a beautiful blue and white sky, with a blue ocean. Ocean waves rising and lowering in a majestic kind of way. The sound of seagulls in the background.

It is Joshua, who has Courtney's hand. He leads her, to his Dad. She holds a bouquet of white roses, green flowers, with long runners of white silk, falling from the bouquet. Her dress is a white silk, like the runners, but with lots of little hand sown beads around the neckline and on the cuffs of the sleeves. It is all lace on the upper chest, shoulders and arms. She looks beautiful!

Joshua then stands behind Elder Hightown. Sitting on the front row is Timothy, with his wife, Emily.

Emily is leaning into Timothy, as he has his arm around the back of her chair. Their daughter Cenya is standing behind Mary, with a bouquet like Mary's.

The Pastor steps forward to stand in front of Aaron and Courtney. He starts off saying "We are gathered here today, to join this man and this women in Holy Matrimony. If anyone has any objections, speak now or forever hold your peace." No one says anything. Both Courtney and Aaron look at each other once again, with that look of love and smile!

glory j mitz

Thank You Father GOD!

CHAPTER 5: My Testimony

November 3, 2003

I SAW THE LIGHT...

I hadn't shared with anyone my testimony of what happened to me, in a long time When it first happened, I found myself talking to everyone about it, all the time, as it severely frighten me. I didn't understand what had happened to me. For about 2 weeks, I could not sleep in my bed. I slept on my living room couch, because I thought it would happen again and this time I would not wake up.

For a long time, I believed what others would tell me about the "I saw the light" experience I had. Some would say, oh I had that experience too, it was probably just a dream. Others would say, we must make sure it wasn't Satan, as he comes as a light bearer. Then there is this one: lots of people have an out of body experience. Which I have come to believe is true.

I realize I will have different reactions to this, from the reaction of the three people I was close to at that time, as I tried to explain to them, what happened to me. Each reacted differently, when I tried to explain, something had happened to me and I didn't understand it.

I do know now that it wasn't just a dream. It was real. I was given a second chance (not sure why me), but at this point what matters is that I be obedient and share my testimony. I do know that if I had been allowed to stay dead (bodily), at that point, I would not have made it into Heaven.

Even though I was going to church and worked on a few committees, I don't think I would have made it in. Not that I was a bad person, but you see I really didn't know who Jesus Christ was. I had not fully excepted him as my Lord and Savior. I do Thank God for his Grace and Mercy, for now I know I do have access to Everlasting Life and Heaven. Praise be to GOD, MY LORD AND SAVIOR, JESUS CHRIST.

Just for the record, these are some of the first people I talked to about my experience. My foster mother: Queen, my son: William and my co-worker, who was a Christian. These three all within the same day or early morning, that same day.

Then, there were a couple of Pastors and Ministers. This was over a few years, as it bothered me that much. I could not rest until I understood what had happened. I needed to know what happened to me, because it was more than a dream. One of the Pastors gave me some insight.

WHAT HAPPENED TO ME

On November 3rd, 2003, I was doing my usual routine. I left work (I worked in RTP) headed to Chavis Park, Raleigh NC. I walked every day around the track at Chavis Park. I knew most of the people there as I was there 7 days a week. I rarely missed going out to walk at Chavis Park.

I remember speaking to one of the men I knew, who was always out there and few other people. This day I did my walk, then drove to Subway in Walnut Creek Shopping Center. I got a half of seafood sub, then drove home to Crestwood Drive in Garner, NC.

I ate my sub, watched TV from about 8 to 10pm. I went to bed, planning to read my bible, until I fell asleep. It was the same routine each night, but November 3rd, 2003 was different. It completely changed me and my life.

Sometime in the night I was awaken, but it was not like I woke up. I could not open my eyes or move my body, but I had the ability to think, because I had this thought: **I've lost my body**. It was like slipping out of a suit and I could not go back in. I could not stop the sensation of "being pulled upward".

I had this sensation of being pulled straight up in the air, very quickly. Extremely fast, I could not make it stop.

Suddenly, I was just hanging there, in mid-air. It wasn't dark, it appeared to be light gray. From what I could see, I did not look the same. I had on a grayish, white garment and I didn't have legs. My body or garment came together at the bottom like a point.

My hands were different too. I had 3 digits - not five fingers. It was as if the middle 3 digits were one, so my thumb had formed a digit, the 3 middle fingers were together and formed another digit, then the small finger, formed the 3rd digit. So, 3 in total, on each hand.

As I was hanging there, I started to get this warm feeling, like lying in the sun, on a bright sunny day. I looked to my right, and there came up this bright light. It came up very slowly. I then heard these words, "Your Blessed". That bright light then went down very, very slowly.

Then behind me, down this very dark tunnel, was a light. I don't know why I looked that way, but I could see it, it was at the end of that tunnel. My whole body started to turn towards that light. I didn't do it, it just started to go that way.

Then I woke up! I just woke up.

When I woke up, I was in my bed. I didn't wake up coughing or choking or having to catch my breath. I previously had a couple of episodes where I woke up having to catch my breath, I knew I had sleep apnea. There was no choking or coughing or grasping for air, this time, I just woke up. I know for sure now, I was sent back. GOD sent me back!

It scared me so bad, as I realized, something different had happened to me. I truly believe I stopped breathing in my sleep. I believe I died, and GOD sent me back.

It frightened me so bad, I could not sleep in my bed for about 2 weeks. I slept on my living room couch, with lots of pillows. That morning, early, as I couldn't go back to slept. I was, to frighten to try to go back to sleep. I called two people. First, I called my foster mother, Queen. I explained to her just what I have explained to you. These were her words to me, "Don't worry about it, it's going to be OK."

That is all she said. I got the feeling she didn't know what to think, me calling her in the middle of the night and telling her all this. We never talked about it again.

I also, called my son, who was not a Christian at the time. This is what he said to me, "Mom you need to go get your hair done or get your nails done. You need to get out more." I realized he didn't understand either what had happened to me.

Next, I talked with my coworker, who was a good friend at work, at the time. I told her everything that had happened and when I got to the part about "Your Blessed", this is what she said, "Don't you think there are somethings you need to do before you can be blessed?"

I didn't understand her anger, because I was still new to the Christian faith, I wasn't saved until 2001, and I was asking her to help me. To explain what happened to me. She always had her bible out at work.

I was expecting her to know and understand, what I went through. She didn't seem to understand. She seemed mad at what I had shared with her. We really didn't talk much after that. I did tell several other people about what happened to me after that, as I stated earlier.

One of the Pastors gave me an answer that helped me understand. He said I had a Damascus Road experience. So, I read up on what happen to Paul in the bible on the Damascus Road and I believe I had an encounter with our risen Lord.

GOD sent me back. I am truly Thankful as I know now, that I would not have made it into Heaven, because I didn't really know Jesus Christ as my LORD AND SAVIOR. I really didn't have a good understanding of who he was until after all this happened, even though, I was in church and working on a few committees. One day it came to me that Jesus is my LORD AND SAVIOR! It was like a light bulb really did come on.

glory mitz

Recently, I had been witnessing to an older gentleman at the nursing home where my foster mother lives. I made the comment to him that I know I died, and GOD was merciful to me and send me back. I told him I wasn't sure why me, why it happened to me, but I was Thankful, that GOD sent me back.

A couple of days later, I woke up with these words on my mind: I've been forgiven. My LORD is risen, and I came back just to let you know.

As I was finishing this, I got these words: the old fall off, so there is new LIFE!

To God Be The Glory, Honor and Praise, Forever!

Amen

Have A Blessed Day! glory j mitz...

www.ingramcontent.com/pod-product-compliance
Lightning Source LLC
Chambersburg PA
CBHW072228190626
46809CB00017B/1528
* 9 7 8 0 5 7 8 4 0 7 4 9 4 *